D0913175

FOLLOW THAT PUPPY!

by Brian Mangas
illustrated by R.W. Alley

SIMON & SCHUSTER BOOKS FOR YOUNG READERS
Published by Simon & Schuster
New York • London • Toronto • Sydney • Tokyo • Singapore

C.10-6-1992

E
man
c.1
90891

SIMON & SCHUSTER BOOKS FOR YOUNG READERS
Simon & Schuster Building, Rockefeller Center
1230 Avenue of the Americas, New York, New York 10020.

Text copyright © 1991 by Brian Mangas.
Illustrations copyright © 1991 by R. W. Alley.
All rights reserved including the right of reproduction
in whole or in part in any form.
SIMON & SCHUSTER BOOKS FOR YOUNG READERS
is a trademark of Simon & Schuster.

The text of this book is set in 14 pt. Impressum.
The display type is Zoro.
The illustrations were done in watercolor and ink.
Designed by Vicki Kalajian

Manufactured in the United States of America

10   9   8   7   6   5   4   3   2   1

Library of Congress Cataloging-in-Publication Data
Mangas, Brian. / by Brian Mangas; illustrated by R. W. Alley.
Follow that puppy!   Summary: Grandpa gets more
than he bargained for when he tries to take a frisky puppy
for a walk.   [1. Dogs—Fiction.   2. Grandfathers—Fiction.]
I. Alley, R. W., ill.   II. Title.   PZ7.M312644Fo   1991   [E]—dc20   90-33877   AC
ISBN 0-671-70780-9

Grace 12.462

For Pam Pollack
BRM

To Grace, with thanks
RWA

"I'm taking the puppy for a walk,"
Grandpa said.

"You'd better not," Grandma warned. "He's too frisky for you. He'll tire you out."

"No, he won't," Grandpa said. "We're only going around the block."

"Okay, go ahead if you want to," Grandma said, "but don't let him get loose."

"Don't be silly," Grandpa said. "I know how to walk a dog."

Grandpa hooked the leash
to Puppy's collar and they
went for a walk.

Puppy pulled on the leash, but Grandpa
held on tightly.
"You can pull all you want," Grandpa said
to Puppy, "but you'll never get away from me."

Puppy pulled this way and that.
He sniffed at everything in sight, but
Grandpa was too strong for him.

"You might as well give up,"
Grandpa said to Puppy. "You're
too little to get away from me,
but I would appreciate it if
you'd relax for a while. Then
we can have a peaceful walk,"
Grandpa added.

Puppy crawled under some bushes.
Grandpa followed.

Puppy ran through a field.
Grandpa held on.

Puppy climbed hills.
"Slow down," Grandpa said.
Puppy crossed streams.
"That's enough," Grandpa cried.
"We're going home."
But Puppy pulled all the more.

"I'll show you who's boss," Grandpa said. Grandpa gave the leash a good strong pull to stop Puppy.

The leash broke and
Puppy was loose.

"Oh, no!" Grandpa cried.

Grandpa jumped into a taxi.
"Follow that puppy," Grandpa said.

The taxi driver took off after Puppy.
He drove too fast and a policeman
pulled him over.

"What's the rush?" the policeman asked.
Grandpa told him about the runaway puppy.

"Come with me," the policeman said.
Grandpa jumped into the police car.

The policeman chased Puppy.
He turned on his red light and
blasted his siren.

Puppy ran into a tunnel.
The policeman and Grandpa followed him.
"Calling all cars, calling all cars," the policeman
said. "Puppy is in the tunnel."

Meanwhile, other policemen were ready to catch Puppy when he came to the end of the tunnel. They set up a big net with ropes, but Puppy was so small that he went right through the net.

The policemen got
tangled up trying to
catch him.
  "Now what'll we do?"
Grandpa asked.
  "They'll stop him
at the bridge,"
the policeman said.

When they got to the bridge,
it looked as if Puppy was trapped,
but he ran past the policemen and
went up the cable to the highest
part of the bridge.

Grandpa went after him.
"Stay," Grandpa shouted,
but Puppy kept going.

Grandpa chased
Puppy up to the
tippy top and finally
caught him.

Then the policeman
helped Grandpa and
Puppy get down.

He took them home and Grandpa
thanked him.
Grandpa and Puppy went inside.

"We're home," Grandpa said as he sat down.
"Hello, dear," Grandma called.
"How was your walk?"
    Grandpa didn't answer.

Grandma went in to see him. He was fast asleep
on the couch.
"I knew you'd tire him out," she said to Puppy,
"but I didn't think a walk around the block
would put him to sleep."

DATE DUE

999